CAT'S WITCH

TIGER series

Damon Burnard	*Revenge of the Killer Vegetables*
Lindsay Camp	*Cabbages from Outer Space*
Mick Fitzmaurice	*Morris Macmillipede*
Elizabeth Hawkins	*Henry's Most Unusual Birthday*
Kara May	*Cat's Witch*
	Cat's Witch and the Lost Birthday
	Cat's Witch and the Monster
	Cat's Witch and the Wizard
	Tracey-Ann and the Buffalo
Barbara Mitchelhill	*The Great Blackpool Sneezing Attack*
Penny Speller	*I Want to be on TV*
Robert Swindells	*Rolf and Rosie*
John Talbot	*Stanley Makes It Big*
Joan Tate	*Dad's Camel*
Hazel Townson	*Amos Shrike, the School Ghost*
	Blue Magic
	Snakes Alive!
	Through the Witch's Window
Jean Wills	*Lily and Lorna*
	The Pop Concert
	The Salt and Pepper Boys

CAT'S WITCH

Kara May

Illustrated by Doffy Weir

Andersen Press · London

For Natasha
Her First Witch

Text © 1990 by Kara May
Illustrations © 1990 by Doffy Weir

First published in 1990
by Andersen Press Limited,
20 Vauxhall Bridge Road, London SW1V 2SA.
This edition published 2002.

British Library Cataloguing in Publication Data available
ISBN 0 86264 274 4

Typesetting by Print Origination (NW) Limited, Formby, Liverpool L37 8EC
Printed and bound in China

1

WHOOSH!

Cat went flying through the air. He went flying through the air on a broomstick. Driving the broomstick was a witch.

Cat was a witch's cat and his witch's name was Aggie.

As witches go, Aggie was the real thing. She was tall and thin and her hair was long and straggly. She wore a pointed hat and a flowing cloak with her name written on them in stardust. Her feet were on the large size – size 17 in shoes. And her nose curved in a magnificent hook that glowed at the tip when she was angry.

As for Cat, he looked like any other cat except for his eyes - which were red.

He'd been with Aggie since he was a kitten. They'd been roaming the skies for years and years. But now they were looking for a house.

'It's time to settle down. I want to live in a house. I want a house of my own,' said Cat's witch Aggie.

Saying she wanted a house of her own was one thing!

Finding a house that Aggie liked was something else! She found something wrong with every one they looked at.

7

'No stairs,' said Aggie. 'I want
a house with stairs in.'

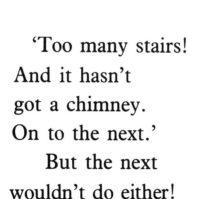

'Too many stairs!
And it hasn't
got a chimney.
On to the next.'
    But the next
wouldn't do either!

8

'Too big!' cried Aggie.

'Then what about that?' said
Cat. 'You can't say that's too big!'

'It's a tent!' screeched Aggie.
'Witches don't live in tents!'

'What sort of house do you
want?' asked Cat, after they'd
looked at house one hundred
and one.

'I don't know what I want. But I
do know I'll know when I see it.'

'I like roaming about here, there and everywhere. I don't know why we have to live anywhere.'

'Because I say,' said Aggie.

'What about me?' scowled Cat. 'What about what I say? You don't care about that!'

'Moan! Moan! Always moaning!' scoffed Aggie.

Cat twitched his whiskers and glowered at Aggie's back.

'Always what *she* says! Never what *I* say! Oh no, indeed!'

He was chuntering away to himself when the broomstick gave a sudden jerk.

'Hey, Cat! Look!'

Down below was a small new town plonked in the middle of nowhere. All around were woods and fields as far as Cat could see.

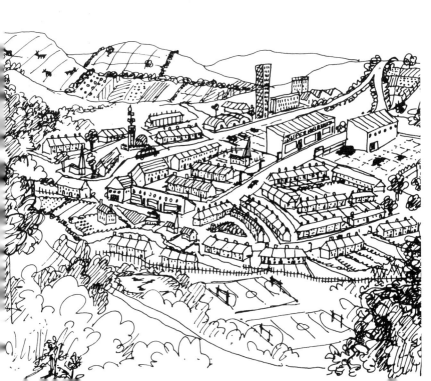

'That's it! That's the place for me!' cried Aggie.

'You've said that a million times before. Then you change your mind,' said Cat.

'This time's different. I feel it in my bones. Now hold your tongue and hold tight, we're going down!'

Aggie was in such a hurry, she sent the broomstick into a nose-dive!

W
  H
    E
      E
        E!

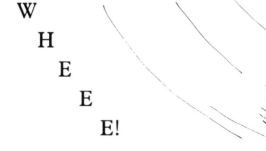

Cat saw the ground coming fast towards him.

'Slow down, Aggie!'

Too late.

The broomstick landed with a
BUMP!

Cat turned head over heels.
BUMPITY BUMP!

That was his head!

'Not one of our best landings!'
said Aggie.

Slowly Cat picked himself up.
Then he exploded:

'Just as well I've got nine lives! I
need them flying with you! One
crash landing after another. How
you got your flying licence I'll
never know.'

'Oh, fiddle - dee - dee! Don't
start your moaning!' said Aggie.

She looked round to see where
they were. She had meant to land
in the town. But somehow she had
landed in a mucky and muddy
field.

'Pick your paws up, Cat, and let's get walking!'

Cat gave her a stony look.

'I'm not walking a step till I've cleaned my coat. Some of us don't like walking around as if we've just had a mud bath! Even if we have!'

'Some of us like fussing about nothing!' snapped Aggie. 'Now let's get going. I'll carry the spoon.'

Aggie tucked her magic spoon
into her hat and marched off
across the field towards the road,
leaving Cat to carry the
broomstick, the pot and the trunk
they kept their bits and bobs in.

'Why can't we go on the
broomstick? I'm not a donkey!'
he raged.

'I want to have a good look
round,' said Aggie.

'There you go again!' said Cat.
'Always what *you* say!'

But Aggie wasn't listening.

'Owls and asps! Look! Look! Look!'

Just ahead was a signpost pointing to the road ahead.

WANTWICH
New Town

'A new town, and it wants a witch!' shrieked Aggie in glee. 'Well, if they're *very* lucky, I might just agree to stay there.'

'They haven't asked you to yet!'

'Still sulking, are we?' grinned Aggie. 'Well, they *will* ask me, you'll see. Witches are hard to come by these days, especially witches like me.'

Then she picked up her skirts and danced round the signpost, round and round, chanting at the top of her voice:

'Wantwich wants a witch
A witchetty witchetty witch!
Which witchetty witch does
                Wantwitch want?
It's Aggie the Witch which
                Wantwitch wants
I'm witchetty as can be!'

She said it over and over, faster and faster, till the words whizzed into each other.

'See if you can say it as fast I can!' cried Aggie.

'I don't want to say it at all,' stormed Cat. 'You're behaving like a two-year-old child, not a hundred-year-old witch! I'm ashamed to be seen with you,' he hissed. 'Dancing and prancing and leaping about! What will people think!'

'There's no one here to think anything!' retorted Aggie. 'But these Wantwichers need to learn how to spell!'

She raised her wand.

ZOOM!

A 'T' jumped in between 'I' and the 'C'.

'You can't do that!' Cat was a-bristle with indignation. 'You can't go round writing on other people's signposts!'

Aggie glared.

'When you're not moaning, you're fussing! Now let's get to Wantwich. Hop on the broomstick.'

'But you said we had to walk!'

'A witch can change her mind, can't she! Stand by Wantwich! Here we come!' cried Cat's witch Aggie.

2

Wantwich was a brand new town, and the people of Wantwich loved it. The houses had gardens for the children to play in. There were smart shops to shop in and three churches and a mosque to choose from. On the edge of the town was a splendid park with a lake in the middle and a fine assortment of ducks.

'We don't get no riff-raff here!' said the Head Duck, who was as proud of the town as the people.

They were so proud of Wantwich
they wore badges, caps, T-shirts
and scarves that said:
WANTWICH IS WONDERFUL
WANTWICH IS BEST
Major Boris Bumpus wrote:
I LOVE WANTWICH
in tulips in his garden. They
came up every spring and made a
spectacular display.

The Wantwichers were a
curious lot. They were the sort of
people who liked to know who was
doing what, where and why, and
they stared at the slightest thing.

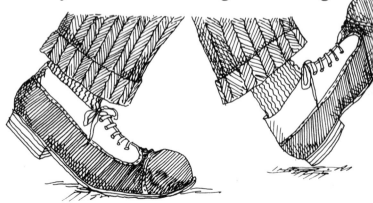

If Mr Macknop, Manager of Sunnivale Supermarket, wore a pair of squeaky shoes, they stared.

If Dr Grimble bought a new car, they stared.

So when a stranger in a pointed hat and a long black cloak came flying down on a broomstick with a cat with red eyes sitting behind her - they gawped and gaped and ooh'd and ahhh'd.

25

'A witch! A witch! It's a witch!' gasped little Ali Shah.

Aggie picked herself up from the ground and gave a friendly smile as wide as a brand new moon.

'The name is Aggie and this here is Cat.'

'We can see it's a cat,' sniffed Major Bumpus.

'Not *a* cat,' Aggie snapped. 'He's *the* Cat! *My* Cat!'

'I'm the cat's whiskers,' drawled Cat.

'That's enough from you,' said Aggie. Then she turned to the Wantwichers. 'Now what houses have you got for me to look at? And don't think any old house will do because it won't.'

'She's fussy about where she lives,' said Cat.

The Wantwichers gave a startled cry.

'You can't live here!'

'You wouldn't fit in!' cried Mr Macknop.

'If a big lump like you fits in, there's room for a slip of a witch like me.'

'That's not the point,' said Mr Macknop's wife, Gloria. 'The point is we don't want your sort in Wantwich.'

Then all the Wantwichers shouted:

'Witch, go away! We don't want you!'

The smile left Aggie's face.
The friendly eyes turned cold.
And her nose began to glow.

'Why do you call your town "Wantwich" if you don't want a witch? Some of my brain magic wouldn't come amiss, if you ask me.'

'That's right, Aggie! You tell them!' cried Cat.

'Now clear off, the lot of you, before I turn you into witchetty grubs.'

Aggie's nose was burning like a furnace. Cat's red eyes were burning like coals.

The Wantwichers took one look at them, turned on their heels and fled.

Cat was quivering with rage. He got fed up with Aggie himself from time to time. But Aggie was his witch and woe betide anyone who said a word against her.

'Put a spell on them, Aggie.
Turn them into rats.'

'I'll sort them later,' said
Aggie. 'But right now I'm going
to look for a house. We're
staying, whether they like it or
not!'

Off they went, all round

Wantwich, knocking at the doors
and calling:

'Does anyone live here?'

Each time the answer was the
same:

'Yes! Go away! We don't want
you!'

Aggie sank wearily down on
the side of the road.

'It's no good, Cat. There's no
house for us here.'

'We're not giving up. You want
to live in Wantwich, and live here
you shall.'

'But all the houses have
someone in them.'

'Maybe that one hasn't.'

Cat pointed to the end of the road
that led to the edge of a wood.

32

Rising above the trees Aggie
spied a roof-top.

'It must have a house! Come
on, let's look!'

She lifted her skirts and raced
down the road.

Peeping through some bushes
of wild white roses was a little

wooden gate. Aggie opened it and
ran on down the ragged little path.

There before them was a little

house. It wasn't new like the other
houses in the town.

'It looks even older than me!'
she said, and knocked on the door.

'Does anyone live here?'

No reply.

Suddenly, there
was a gust of wind.

SSSSSSSSSH!

The door opened with a loud
CREAK, and Cat and Aggie
peered inside.

The room before them was
empty. Dust covered the floor
and cobwebs hung from the
ceiling. But Aggie jumped up and
down in delight.

'There's a fireplace for cooking my spells! And even a hole in the roof! It's like having an airport in the house. I can fly straight up to the sky!'

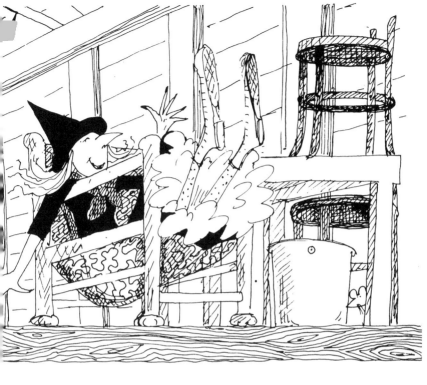

'And what, pray, do we do
when it rains?'

'Catch the water in a bucket, of
course. Now let's see what else
we can find.'

In the attic they found some
furniture:

a bed with three legs

a big chair with a saggy bottom

two small chairs with no backs
a bucket with no handle
a table with an inkstand in the
shape of a rose.

Aggie was thrilled.

'Everything a witch could want!
This is the house for me. Do say
you like it, Cat. Not that it makes
any difference,' she added.

Cat sniffed.

'It's got a friendly
smell to it, I'll say
that for it. I suppose
I could live here -
once it's had a
good clean.'

'Fuss! Fuss! Fuss! It's fine as it is!' said Aggie.

Cat gave her a very firm, stern look.

'Now look here. I don't want to live in a house. I'm only doing it because *you* want to. The least you can do is clean it up.'

'If I must, I suppose I must,' sighed Aggie. 'I'll look up a house-cleaning spell.'

'Oh no you don't!' cut in Cat. 'More often than not, it takes you ten times to get a spell right, and it's almost dark. Maybe you can sleep surrounded by dirt and dust and rubbish and rubble, but I can't. Call me fussy if you like but - '

'All right, all right, don't go on,' said Aggie.

'Come on then, let's get started.'

Aggie and Cat set to. Or rather, Cat did! While Aggie wandered around with a duster,

Cat got down on all paws and
scrubbed and polished till the
little house shone.

Aggie danced around in glee.

'Oh Cat! What bliss! Such a
dear little house! What a lucky
witch I am, I am!'

But just then, there was a loud
KNOCK! KNOCK! KNOCK!
on the door.

It was Mr Macknop.

'That's my house!' he roared.
'Get out!'

'You're not living here,'
shouted Aggie.

'I live in another house,'
shouted back Mr Macknop.

'You can't live in two houses at
once! I'll pay a fair price for this
one, but not a penny more.'

'I'm not selling it to you!'

'Think about it!' screeched Aggie.

'I don't need to think about it!' bellowed Mr Macknop.

'Good, then that's settled. I'll pay you in the morning.'

Before Mr Macknop could say another word, Aggie flew back indoors.

'I smell trouble,' said Cat.

'If trouble comes, I'll send it back where it came from, never you fear!' said Cat's witch Aggie.

3

The next morning, the sun shone bright. Sunbeams danced on Aggie's bedroom wall.

'Good morning, Sunbeams!' she cried, as she leapt out of bed.

'Someone's in a good mood this morning,' said Cat, with a yawn and stretch.

'Our little house! My dream house!' cried Aggie. 'But a house isn't a home till it has a name. What shall we call it?'

While they were thinking, their ears began to burn.

Cat and Aggie looked at each other.

'Someone's talking about us!' they said.

'Listen,' said Aggie.

'I'm listening,' said Cat.

In the shopping centre, the Wantwichers were having a meeting. A meeting about Aggie and Cat.

'That old bat of a witch! What a scruff!'

'And that spiteful looking cat!'

'We don't want them in Wantwich!'

'We'll throw them out!'

'By hook or by crook we'll get them out!'

'Aggie and Cat! Out! Out! Out!'

The Wantwichers didn't know that Aggie and Cat had the power to hear every word that was said about them. When the words were mean and nasty, their ears began to burn. And right now, their ears were burning like bonfires.

Aggie leapt up.

'How dare they!'

Cat's fur was bristling.

'Spiteful! Me! I'm the kindest and sweetest of cats!'

'And I'm the kindest and sweetest of witches! Until I'm crossed that is.'

Her eyes gleamed.

'I'll teach these Wantwichers a lesson! A lesson they'll never forget!'

She gave a chuckle like pebbles rattling in an old tin can.

'Never again shall they take the names of Aggie the Witch and Cat in vain! I shall take their voices away, that's what! Fetch the spell book! Put on the pot!'

49

'As said is done!' cried Cat.
While Cat lit the fire, Aggie
looked up the spell.

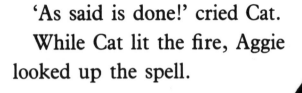

SPELL FOR
TAKING AWAY
VOICES
INGREDIENTS:
3 slugs
1 toad
5 worms
2 spiders
1 mouse.

'Make sure they're dead ones,
Cat. I don't like using live
creatures in my spells. I'm too
kind-hearted.'

'You mean they keeping jumping out of the pot and you can't be bothered to catch them!' said Cat.

'Off with you! Or you'll find your voice in the pot with the rest!'

At last everything was ready.
Aggie took her magic spoon from
under her hat and stirred the pot.
Cat stood by, making a strange
cry that he only used for spells,
while Aggie chanted the magic
rhyme:

     'Wantwitch voices, come this way
     Jump in the pot without delay!

Hecate Hecuba
Hullabaloo
Jiggery Pokery
Wizamaroo
Hocus pokus
Fi fo fum
Abracadabra
The spell is done.'

In no time at all, the pot was
bubbling with voices. Cat banged
down the lid so they couldn't escape.

'Now,' said Aggie, 'let's see how the spell is working.'

She whistled for the broomstick and they flew to the shopping centre.

People were rushing around in a panic.

They opened their mouths and shut their mouths.

They twisted their faces from side to side.

They put out their tongues and looked at their tonsils.

'Morning, everyone! Lovely day!' cried Aggie.

Everyone stared and glared, but nobody spoke.

'Seems they've lost their voices,' said Cat.

'They don't deserve to have them,' said Aggie. 'Voices are precious gifts, not to be wasted on cruel words about strangers.'

Then to show how much voice *she* had, Aggie began to sing:

'I'm Aggie the Witch
The Wantwich witch
The witch that's spelt with a "t".
I've got your voices in my pot
Bubble and boil, I've got the lot!
They all belong to me.'

She marched all round the town, singing her loudest with Cat caterwauling beside her.

'Now we'll be off,' said Aggie at last. 'I need some cloud-water for a spell.'

At the word 'spell' the Wantwichers turned pale. On trembling legs they rushed off to their houses.

'Are you going to put another spell on them?' asked Cat, as they zoomed into the sky.

'Wait and see,' said Aggie.

And would say no more.

They had to fly out to sea to find a cloud. Cat collected a few drops of water in a little silver box, then they headed back to Wantwich.

'Look, Aggie!' he cried.

Outside the gate of the little house stood all the people of Wantwich. They didn't look rude and uppity now!

Quivering and shaking with
fearful faces, Mr Macknop and
Dr Grimble stepped forward
with a large blackboard.

'What have we here?' said Cat's
witch Aggie.

She whistled up her specs to
read what it said:

URGENT
Dear Aggie and Cat,
We are very sorry we were so rude
and unkind. We hope you will
forgive us.

Signed: THE PEOPLE OF
WANTWICH.

P.S. If you could find it in
your hearts to give us back
our voices, we would be
very very grateful.

Aggie turned thoughtfully to Cat.

'I can remember the spell for taking voices *away* . . .'

'Easy as pie!' said Cat.

'But I seem to have forgotten the spell for giving them back.'

'That would take a lot of remembering.'

'About £50 worth,' said Aggie.

The Wantwichers reached for their pockets. Cat collected the money in Aggie's hat.

'Spells work much quicker if the pot has a house to live in,' went on Aggie. 'I wonder how much this house is?'

Mr Macknop rushed to the blackboard and wrote:

'Fifty pounds to you, Aggie.'

'Done! Give him the money, Cat. Now,' said Aggie, 'I'll see if I can remember that spell.'

Cat poked up the fire.

'What do we need for the spell, Aggie?'

'Just a few drops of rainwater!' was Aggie's reply.

Cat roared with laughter.
'You knew they'd say sorry!
You crafty old Aggie Witch!'
'That's as maybe,' said Aggie.
She lifted the lid and Cat
dropped the cloud-water into the
pot.

The voices jumped out, and went back where they'd come from. Then all together they let out a cheer:

'Welcome to Wantwich, Aggie and Cat!'

Then the Wantwichers came running down the path with friendly smiles and house-warming presents.

'A home of our own and friends to go with it! Oh what a happy witch I am, I am!' beamed Aggie.

'It's not a home yet. Not till it's got a name,' said Cat.

Then WHHHT! a name popped into his head!

'Roof Hole House! How does that sound?'

'It sounds just right!' said Cat's witch Aggie.

And there they lived, in Roof Hole House, for years and years to come.